Kendra Temples:
The Demonic Diaries Vol. 2

HELLCRAFTER

Eve Harms

ISBN: 9781703796223

For content warnings go to the last page
eveharms.com

To anyone who's lost someone

2018

June

Using Flotation Hallucinations for Writing Inspiration (and to Visit the Dead?!?)

Posted by Kendra Temples on June 21st, 2018

I'm obsessed with traveling to other dimensions. In my quest for writerly inspiration I came across flotation tanks. You know—Stranger Things, Fringe, Altered States and all that? They all feature flotation tanks, sometimes calling them isolation tanks. And no, I'm not traveling to The Upside Down or turning into a caveman, but I am traveling to other dimensions, in my mind and imagination. It's sort of like lucid dreaming, but I'm not exactly in control. Well, I guess “not exactly in control" is kind of the norm for me.

I go to this float spa named Float Void to practice my inter-dimensional travel. The process is like this: you get a small private room with a shower and flotation tank–the tanks at Float Void are pretty roomy, and I can stretch my arms all the way out. The tank is completely dark and filled with body temperature salt water. You put in earplugs, and your senses are blocked out so your mind can roam free in the womb-like space. I've been trying to induce hallucinations while floating and yesterday I was finally able to immerse myself and explore my mind-space for more than a few seconds.

And you won't believe what I saw.

In the blackness I started to see faint purple swirls. I focused my mind on them and imagined myself walking toward them until I started to enter a trance. It felt like I was really moving my legs and walking toward them. I was probably twitching like a puppy having a bad dream.

As I walked towards the purple swirls, they brightened until they became pure white, like sunlight, and I blocked my eyes with my hand to stop them from stinging.

I could see my hand. I could feel the ground becoming soft under my feet. I could feel the warmth of the light. The light pulsed and softened. I took my hand away from my face.

I was in a desert with orange sand and blood-red skies, straight out of the cover of my dead ex-boyfriend's copy of Frank Herbert's *Dune* that I still haven't finished. Strange plants jutted out from the ground, home to insects that grotesquely shared human features: eyes, teeth, hands, fingernails. A humongous featherless vulture that looked as if it was made of black liquid velvet soared just overhead, and deposited its neon green droppings onto my shoulder. It was freaking awesome, and I mentally patted myself on the back for having such a killer imagination.

I heard a strange elephant-like grunt and turned around to see two figures trudging through the desert. They were accompanied by a buffalo-sized creature that looked like a hairless anteater with a saddle and cargo on top of it. I walked closer and saw they were wearing red cloaks, probably to cover themselves from the harsh sun. Their faces were obscured by the hoods on their cloaks, and their bodies were covered from head to toe with the worn, dirty garments. One of them looked up and I saw his face. It was Steve. My dead ex-boyfriend.

I met him online a few years ago, and we bonded over old cheesy 70s and 80s science-fiction fantasy movies and books. They were the type of old paperbacks with the muscly guy on the cover holding a sword, accompanied by an alien friend who looks like a chimp, and creepy monsters stalking them in a psychedelic landscape. I actually started collecting them recently because they remind me of him, and I've been posting them on my instagram.

Anyways, after I destroyed my life in my hometown, I ended up hitchhiking across the country to L.A. to move in with him. He was kind of a dick, but I loved him. And then I killed him. Well, not exactly. But it was my fault he died.

It's been just over a year since that night, but I still have flashbacks. I see his skin tearing off while he gets sucked into a portal, created by a shaytan (an evil jinn, comparable to a demon) I released named Mhaqal—who possessed my rich boss's wife when I was working as a librarian in his creepy mansion. How's that for a quarter-life crisis?

I thought I'd mostly gotten over losing him. I try not to think about him. But apparently I've been thinking about him more than I realized, because in that other dimension, he was pointing his gloved hand right at me!

He turned to his companion to say something I couldn't hear. Then I saw his companion's face—he lifted his head to talk to Steve, and it emerged out from underneath the cloak. It was the head of the goat! Or maybe a mask?

I yelled at them and tried to get his attention, but he ignored me. Typical. He was probably still mad at me. But then he gestured in my direction. I turned around; he was pointing to craggy towers far into the distance. He couldn't see me. He couldn't hear me. But I could see him.

I walked closer to see if I could hear what they were saying—and then it all vanished. I woke up and I had to pee really bad—so bad it must have knocked me out of the trance.

I'll admit it, I couldn't wait to get dressed and use the bathroom in the hall, so I peed in the shower. Don't judge! I rinsed it out! I bet other customers do it all the time.

I saw Steve. And he had skin! I guess his skin peeling off was just an illusion created by Mhaqal, her little creative flair to put a cherry on top of my trauma. Was this hell? Was this the dimension Mhaqal sent him to, where he's destined to endlessly traverse the desert with no one to talk to but a goat?

What am I talking about? This is all my imagination. Steve's dead and I'll never see him again. I shouldn't be indulging this fantasy that he's still out there somewhere.

But you know what? I don't care. I'm going back into that tank as soon as I can.

You Won't Believe What I Saw on Craigslist

Posted by Kendra Temples on June 24th, 2018

Yeah, Craigslist. The same place I got that occult librarian job. The job that got me in this mess in the first place. I might as well blame all of my problems on this "Craig" and his nefarious "list."

But I finally needed a job again. After getting a sweet vintage car (a black 1969 Volvo 144), a new laptop and phone, and spending a year of an otherwise frugal, jobless life as a "writer", I'm nearly broke. Like, "Where's the rent Kendra?" broke. Like, no more floating broke. Like, starting a gargoyle-fetish erotica pen name broke. Don't go Googlin', I didn't actually start one... yet.

You can't blame me for being a bum, though. I went through some seriously traumatic shit! I still get flashbacks and bolts of fear when I see certain insects, snakes, and even white cats. And if I follow you on twitter can you please stop posting those face-melting-off GIFs? Sure, I love horror, but when I see that Indiana Jones and the Temple of Doom GIF it puts me right back in the insectarium where Steve's skin got peeled off, and he was sucked into the portal.

Speaking of Indiana Jones, I relate to the guy: I can't stand snakes now, either. And white kittens make me paranoid. What if Mhaqal is still trapped inside of a white cat and is stalking me, waiting to find the perfect way to ruin my life? Oh, but don't stop posting cat GIFs, please! Those get me through the day.

I'm getting sidetracked. Craigslist. My favorite float spa, Float Void, posted a job. It offers decent pay and free floats. That means more inter-dimensional travel and chances to see Steve—even if it's just my imagination.

So I did the obvious thing: I reported the ad for fraud over and over again so no one else would see it, and went in to fill out an application. And it worked! I got an interview. I'll let you know how it goes.

I Got the Job!

Posted by Kendra Temples on June 28th, 2018

I start on Monday! I'm excited, but Carlos seemed even more excited. I think he's been worried that I've been in a rut—probably because when he visits my eyes are glazed over from too much Netflix, and my clothes and tongue are covered in bright red Hot Cheeto dust.

Oh yeah, I guess I never told you guys about him. Carlos is my boyfriend. We've been dating for nearly 6 months, and it seems like he's getting serious. Am *I* serious? I don't know. I mean, the guy is an absolute gem: kind, supportive, patient, thoughtful, a good listener, and everything else the perfect boyfriend should be. He even bought me chopsticks to help keep the aforementioned Hot Cheeto dust off of the black tank top I never change out of.

And the poor guy puts up with a lot. I can't imagine that my depression, anxiety, and PTSD —plus the weight gain and declining hygiene that go with it—are anyone's version of happily ever after. Why is he so into me? I'm a total mess.

It's just... the passion isn't there. And honestly, I probably wouldn't have gone out with him a second time if he hadn't been the only sane person I'd encountered after a rash of horrible Tinder dates. Maybe I should've written a blog about that... Tales from Tinder!

And the sex isn't great. (TMI alert!) Not only am I not super into him, he's so dang anxious to please me while we do it. He acts like I'm going to pull a revolver out from under the pillow and shoot him in the head if I don't get off. It's a huge turnoff. I know he just wants me to have a good time, but I just wish he'd relax and enjoy himself too, not treat me like the final boss in one of those video games he plays.

Every time I decide I should break it off with him he does something super thoughtful like giving me a bouquet of black roses in a weird head-shaped vase he made in ceramics class, or waking me up with his mom's insanely-good tamales. He didn't even care that I ate them without getting out of bed. He must have some sort of "Kendra's gonna dump me" sixth sense, because it's impossible to let him go after he does something that nice.

And I feel extra-guilty about how excited he is about my new job. His heart would be broken if he knew the real reason I applied was so that I could travel to another dimension to visit my dead ex-boyfriend Steve. Or maybe he'd be confused. Or maybe he'd just think I'm crazy.

What the heck is wrong with me? I've got the perfect guy right in front of me and I'm pining after a dead ex who was frankly kind of an asshole when we were dating. But he's not all bad. I'll admit we had good times that never made it in my blog. Because the good times aren't interesting to read about, right?

I guess I just need to let Steve go. And maybe I shouldn't even take the job. I don't know... what do you guys think?

July

I Have to Tell You What I Saw

Posted by Kendra Temples on July 5th, 2018

I started my job at Float Void, but I'll get into that later. Because what I saw in the tank was seriously f-ed up.

I was able to visit the desert of Hellworld again. Yeah, I know "Hellworld" sounds like a fifth-rate amusement park you only end up at after you've already gone to Disneyland, Universal Studios, Knott's Berry Farm, and Six Flags. But the name almost makes me chuckle, and with how messed up my life is getting, I'll take whatever I can get.

After entering a trance, I opened my eyes to see three bright green serpent-like creatures towering over me. Slime dripped off of the fangs of their mouths, which hung open below their black, bulging, wasp-like eyes. Two insect arms jutted out of their body, jittering with anticipation.

These things probably couldn't hurt me, or even see me, but I turned to run before I could think about that.

When I turned around, I nearly ran into—I mean through—Steve and the goat-man, who were facing off with the beasts with their swords drawn. Behind them was their giant, hairless anteater creature, wounded and lying on its side with their cargo scattered around it. We were all half-surrounded by a sea of pitch black brambles with thorns the size of fingers.

One of them charged at Steve—passing right through me—and he jumped away, slicing at the creature. His sword must've been too blunt as it only knocked it back and caused it to make a sound like a mix between a wet insect buzz and a shriek. He muttered "shit" under his breath.

The creature lunged at Steve, and knocked him over. Its teeth were inches away from his face, until it was sliced in half by the goat-man. The pieces of the serpent-like creature twisted and shook as its guts spilled out in waterfalls of blood. The goat-man walked over the steaming pool of serpentine guts to offer his hand to Steve. "You should keep your blade sharp."

Steve scoffed and said, "Yours is only sharp because you never use it."

Is it just me or did surviving a hellscape for a year give Steve a sort of rugged charm?

He grunted and took the goat-man's hand, but the hairy companion's grip was released when he was knocked over to the ground. The goat-man struggled under the weight of another wasp-eyed-serpent that slashed at his snout with its insectoid arms. I guess we were all too caught up in the snarky action hero banter to remember that there were two other monsters hellbent on slaughter.

The remaining serpents advanced on Steve. He trotted backwards, always facing the creature with his blunt sword up. The beast lunged at him, and Steve hopped out of its way, swinging his blade downward into a squat pumpkin-like plant on the desert floor beside him.

His blade punctured the blood-red veiny bulb. He let go of his sword and covered his face with his cloak, somersaulting away as the pulsating gourd gushed out a geyser of pink liquid onto the wasp-eyed serpent. The serpent squealed and writhed as the sticky goo bubbled against its scaly skin, eating it away. Steve turned to see the goat-man unconscious under the last wasp-eyed serpent.

Steve crouched. He leapt at the creature, and tackled it off the goat-man, sending it rolling to the ground. It kicked up orange dust plumes in its wake. The serpent-thing quickly regained control, lunged at Steve, and bit into his cloaked arm.

Steve shrieked and thrashed, but held his ground and tried to throw it off. I ran over to pull the monster off of him, but my hands phased in and out of its body, barely nudging it. I was going to watch him die again, helplessly, and it was all my fault. He shouldn't be here in the first place. He should be in the real-world with me, watching bad movies and making fun of my poetry.

Steve stopped thrashing and began to push the snake backward towards the thorny black bushes. When the beast was close enough to the tangled brush, Steve charged into the creature with a cry of pain, shifting the beast so that the tip of its tail brushed one of the thorny branches.

The branch instantly came alive and wrapped around the snake's tail, drawing blood. The brambles seemed to be feeding on the blood, and the branches grew outwards, slurping and creaking, as the red liquid was sucked into its pores. The branches pulled the serpent in, along with Steve, whose arm was still in the grip of the serpent's jaws. The two were drawn closer and closer to the dense, hungry brush. The thorny branches grew toward them, longer with every second until they'd engulfed half of the snake, twisting its body and wringing out its bright red blood. Each drop soaked into the dark, porous branches, causing them to elongate and fractalize further. Steve pounded his free fist into the head of the serpent with his eyes squeezed tight. The elongating branches pulled him inches away from the bloodthirsty forest of thorns.

Just as the plant began to wrap around the snake's head and the thorns started to surround and scratch Steve's cloaked arm, Steve slipped his arm out of the cloak and spun around, freeing himself and tumbling on to the ground like a rag doll. The wasp-eyed serpent must've finally lost its grip.

The brambles sucked his cloak into their tangled and spiky web, shredding it and stretching it to pieces, along with the pale, deflated snake carcass. Having no more blood to feed on, the branches became stiff and still once again, not even moving with the breeze.

Steve wiped the sweat off his brow with the long sleeve covering his forearm. The dirty white sleeve had a small but growing bloodstain on it. The cloak must have protected him. He looked to the ground at his unconscious partner. He walked over and gave the goat-man a couple of kicks in the side. "You alive Robert? Wake up."

I guess his name is Robert? Goat-Rob didn't move, so Steve crouched down. "Robert? You okay?"

Steve's brow furrowed. "Come on Robert, this isn't funny. I'm wounded and I need your help setting up the tent..."

Steve felt around Robert's neck, placing two fingers on different spots. "How the fuck do you check a goat's pulse? Robert!"

Panic started to enter his voice. "Wake up Robert! Wake up!"

He raised his hand high to slap the goat-man's face but Goat-Rob's hand quickly shot up and grabbed his wrist. "Please don't slap me."

"Jesus, Robert. You scared the crap out of me. You okay?"

"Just a couple scratches, I'm fine. A story to tell at a bar, if a bar even exists in this godforsaken dimension."

"Did you faint again?"

"I guess it's just my defense mechanism."

Steve scoffed. "That has to be the worst defense mechanism I've ever heard of."

"It's perfect. If I wake up, fine. And if I don't wake up, I'm not alive to know I'm dead."

Steve helped him up with a grunt. They walked over to the giant, hairless anteater who lay dead next to their packs, the contents strewn across the ground. Robert sighed and patted the creature on its side before opening a pack and pulling out a series of bamboo-like rods. Steve told Robert, "It'll only get more dangerous as we get closer to the palace." Was he talking about those craggy towers in the distance?

Steve helped him extend the telescoping rods. "Our chances aren't good with a melted sword and Betsy gone." That must have been the name of their anteater-like creature.

Goat-Rob began to connect the different rods together. "Are we going to bury the poor girl?"

"Yes. But we can't let her body go to waste."

My stomach tightened at the thought of what they were going to do with Betsy's body. The two were silent while they finished setting up the shelter, connecting the last of the rods and draping a canvas cloth over it to form a tent. I wanted to say something or make a stupid joke to break the tension but they wouldn't have been able to hear me. And it's not like my tension breaking jokes have had much success in the past.

I followed Steve into the tent. He couldn't hear me and his back was turned, but I said everything anyways.

I'm so fucking sorry. It was all my fault that you died. And I was a terrible girlfriend to you. I love you and miss you so much. This shouldn't have happened, none of this should've happened. You should be alive. Are you alive, Steve? Are you just somewhere else? Or is this just my imagination?

He pulled up the bottom of his long sleeve shirt to take it off, and revealed naked red muscles held tightly together by white sinews and blue veins bulging out. From the shredded flesh of his neckline down, he was like an anatomical model. But alive. So alive. His muscles rippled and twitched as he moved. His body appeared to be covered in some sort of clear film that must have held him together.

The vision of his skin being pulled off when he slipped into the portal was real. And it flashed before my eyes again.

I screamed. It felt like forever and rang in my ears until it was accompanied by another high-pitched squeal.

My eyes shot open. It was the security alarm at the spa. My co-worker Crash (I'll tell you about him later) must've forgotten I was floating and armed it when he left. How long was I in the tank for, and what set off the alarm?

I forgot how low the ceiling in the tank was, so I bonked my head and fell on my ass before getting out. I grabbed a towel and wrapped myself with it and ran to turn off the alarm. But the police were already knocking on the door. I guess they thought it was pretty funny, finding a shivering girl in only a towel, because even after I proved I was an employee they kept on saying shit like, "We might have to cuff you and take you down to the station, just in case. You look like a bad girl." And "Maybe I'll take you for a ride in the back of my police car." I hate them.

My boss sounded pretty cranky on the phone about it, but that might be because the call woke her up at 3 AM. She said we'll talk about it later. Hopefully I'll still have a job by my next post.

The Life of a Float Spa Attendant

Posted by Kendra Temples on July 8th, 2018

So, I promised I'd tell you guys a bit about my job working at Float Void. No, I didn't get fired for that incident where I set off the alarm and answered the door naked for a bunch of pigs. Hurray for me, right?

Outside of what goes on in the tanks, it's a pretty mellow and simple job. Definitely not as much excitement as working as an occult librarian in a creepy mansion!

I've actually not been floating as much since the last time I found Steve and saw how he was missing all of the skin below his neck. And I haven't been able to project into Hellworld when I do. It's probably for the best. I don't need any extra nightmares about my skinless ex-boyfriend, thank you very much.

But I'm just as anxious about whether he's in danger in that hellish place. I mean, of course he's in danger. Why are he and Goat-Rob going to that craggy palace? Jesus, I'm talking like it's real. You guys must think I'm crazy.

Anyway, I told you I'd write about working at the float spa. Focus, Kendra. The job is pretty mellow. Mostly cleaning and talking to customers, giving them instructions on how to prepare for their float and what to expect when they're in the tank. I usually leave out the part about potentially teleporting to a hell dimension—it might be bad for business.

Most of our customers are pretty chill, way easier than the people who would frequent the tanning salon I used to work at. We've even had a few celebrities float. I won't say who, but one of their names rhymes with "Ridiculous Sage" LOL.

I like my boss and coworkers. Well, it's really just one guy I ever have a shift with, Crash. He's a character, for sure. He's got dirty blonde hair (the color and cleanliness) and wears a drug-rug and these huge billowy hippy pants. If you put him in some normal clothes and gave him a bubble bath he might be kinda cute.

But he's a really nice guy. I hung out at his place last night after work and he told me that he goes on "vision quests" inside the tank. The best journey he had was on acid—a big Float Void no-no. I told him that I haven't been able to have visions in the tank lately, like something is blocking me from "getting in the zone." Crash said LSD would clear the blockage right out, and it could even give me control over the vision, as if I have god-like powers. He offered to get me some.

LSD? I don't know, that sounds scary. I've never done drugs before, not even weed, and an LSD + PTSD combo probably isn't a great way to start.

But if it could help me help Steve, it might be worth the risk. Jesus, I need to get a grip! I just can't help it. Even if it's just my imagination, I want him to be okay. It's not real, right? I'm crazy to think it could be, right? Please tell me I'm crazy.

Sonja Called

Posted by Kendra Temples on July 12th, 2018

I thought I'd never hear from her again. I didn't even know if she was alive. Last I heard she was three months into a coma with little to no brain activity. She said she's been reading my blog, and had something she needed to show me in person. How did she find my blog, anyway? Kendra Temples isn't my real name. Are you reading this now, "Sonja"?

I asked her if she was mad about the blog and she gave me her classic Sonja laugh—three musical hahs. It was a relief to hear a real Sonja laugh. "No, no. I liked your portrayal of me. You didn't use my real name and besides, who would ever believe any of it?"

She had a point. Sometimes I don't even believe it myself. And you guys probably don't believe me either, do you? You think I'm writing fiction or that I'm bonkers. Poor nutty Kendra. That's why I don't talk about it with my boyfriend Carlos and I don't see a therapist. I'm afraid they'd lock me up in the loony bin after hearing my story. If nothing else, I doubt I'd get the type of support I need. "Yes, Kendra. It was the evil genies, not a coping mechanism your psyche created to deal with your missing ex-boyfriend."

So talking with some one who would actually believe me sounded kind of appealing—even though the thought of returning to the mansion filled me with a burning dread.

Every cell in my body screamed "Don't go, don't go, don't go." So for once I listened to my better judgement and told her that I'm sorry and I just couldn't do it and then hung up. Sorry guys, I know that doesn't make for a great story.

But then she texted me. "It's about Steve."

Fuck. Steve. How could it be about Steve?

I've been trying to visit the hell dimension lately. But I still can't keep my concentration long enough to manifest myself there. I'm really hoping he's okay.

What could she possibly have to show me that has to do with Steve? I shouldn't go, right guys?

Return to Eli's Mansion

Posted by Kendra Temples on July 15th, 2018

I drove my black vintage Volvo up the big hill to Eli's mansion A.K.A. Kendra's PTSD Palace. When I pulled up I almost thought I'd come to the wrong house. The flat gray exterior was now baby blue with a clean white trim. It definitely looked less ominous now. Almost generic... as generic as a giant ornate Victorian mansion can be, I guess.

I rung the doorbell. I was expecting Sonja, Eli, or a butler to answer the door, but instead I was greeted by a rail thin girl with light purple hair. Dark purple matte lipstick surrounded her totally fake smile, and a light red smoky eye with winged eyeliner was under her annoyingly flawless brows. She wore a giant cross necklace around her neck held by a thick chain, plus a white jean jacket with a skintight black T-shirt underneath. Who the heck was this girl?

"You must be Kendra," she said, "I've heard so much about you. I'm Andrea. I'm the librarian here."

She's the librarian? I must've looked shocked because she said, “What did you think, they were just going to burn down the library after you left? Well don't just stand there, come on in!"

The previously white walls were painted an ugly light yellow, and the folk art and antiques were replaced by landscapes and pop art. And when I entered the library, I barely recognized it.

The library was brightly lit, spotless and clean, the shelves were refurnished, and the rickety rusted metal catwalk was replaced by a mahogany balcony with a shining wooden staircase to match. Andrea put her arms up as she led me in and then spun around, with a smile. "Ta da! I've made a few changes, when I first got here it was so gross and dark and creepy. Isn't it much more welcoming now?"

I looked around in disbelief at what she'd done to my library. And then I saw what used to be the occult section. The wall hiding it was gone, it was painted in bright basic colors, the shelves were replaced, and it was full of children's books! WTF?

"Where're all the occult books?" I asked.

"Oh, all those creepy books? We got rid of them. Bad vibes, y'know?"

"Where's the secret passageway?" I asked, “You can't have a creepy mansion without a secret passageway! And what the hell is up with all these kiddie books?"

"Kendra?" a familiar voice said from behind me.

I turned around to see Sonja. A very pregnant Sonja. Her previously long messy hair was cut short into a clean bob, and she was wearing a flowing white dress. She was glowing like some sort of pregnant angel.

"Sonja," I said, “Your..."

"Yes," she said with a half smile, “Nearly 8 months.”

“And you look great," I said. It was a relief to see the same old Sonja, with more color in her skin and more strength and presence.

"Where's Eli?"

"Eli's filming in Australia. We can catch up later. Andrea, could you bring me the book you found?"

Andrea went to her overly tidy desk and picked up a paperback. She handed it to me. It was one of those old pulp science-fiction fantasy paperbacks—like the ones I've been collecting and posting on my Instagram. The ones that remind me of Steve. On the cover there were two figures in a surreal desert landscape, a man with a goat's head, and a human. They looked just like Steve and Goat-Rob. The title: *Journey to the Hellworld.* The Author: H.Q. Alma. The publication year: 1979.

"It's from the original collection of the library," said Andrea, "When Eli bought the mansion there were already a ton of books here. Pretty cool, huh? Sonja said that you liked old paperbacks like these."

Sonja stared at me with her piercing eyes, "I saw the cover and I thought you might like to have it."

What. The. Freaking. Hell. I was seriously beginning to question my sanity—and I haven't stopped questioning it yet, honestly.

I asked Sonja if I could talk to her in private.

She agreed and led me to the kitchen to join her in the breakfast nook for some tea. Tea? Freaking tea? This was not a tea-time discussion.

She came out of the kitchen with the steaming glasses of tea and a concerned look on her face—she must have saw me shaking. “Please, drink this. It will calm you down.”

I took a sip: a moment to clear my thoughts. I had to start from the beginning, when Mhaqal sent Steve into that portal. Maybe Sonja shared Mhaqal’s thoughts and knew more about where that portal went to. “Were you... were you conscious when you were possessed by Mhaqal?"

Tears welled up in her eyes, "I'm so sorry Kendra. Most of the time I was conscious. Sometimes I felt in control, sometimes I could feel Mhaqal controlling my actions, and sometimes I couldn’t tell the difference. But that night I was experiencing one of my blackouts.”

"It's okay. I guess that’s what happens when you’re possessed.”

"I think Mhaqal lived quietly in me so long, draining my resolve and my vitality. Making me sick, poisoning my body and mind. A stronger person could've fought against it."

I gave her a long hug—I needed one just as much as her—and when we sat back down I said, “So, you've been reading my blog?"

"Yes, your stories about Steve are just like the stories in the book Andrea found."

"You read the whole thing? How... how does it end?"

Sonja's gaze fell before it met mine again. “It ends on a cliffhanger. I’m not sure if it’s supposed to be a series or not. It doesn’t look great for Steve toward the end, but there’s no way to know how it turns out.”

My brain sunk into my skull and my eyes started to water. I was going to lose him again. Sonja grabbed my hand, bringing my gaze back to her piercing eyes. "Kendra. Change the course of Steve's story. Save him."

"I thought it was all in my imagination. I'm just a projection in Hellworld, I can't do anything to help him."

"You have to try. What if the author never wrote the next book, and Steve’s story isn’t set in stone?”

"Or I'll just keep going back to Hellworld, helplessly watching him suffer and die, over and over.”

"Reality and meta-reality is malleable, you know this. We live in a hologram. Everything has many sides."

I thanked Sonja and headed home, grateful to get out of that place. We'd bonded on theories of reality in the past but I couldn't really deal with that crap right now. At the time it was fun to think about that stuff. But when you can barely get a grip on your own subjective reality? Not so much.

That girl Andrea gave me her number and told me the two of us should hang out. What's her deal? Why would she want to hang out with me?

I should probably quit my job at the float spa, and stop visiting Hellworld. This can't end well. And I can't bear to go through what I went through in the insectarium again. Maybe I should burn that book too. It's right next to me as I write this post. I've been too scared to read it yet, if I do, and if what Sonja says is true, it makes all of this real. Or proves that I'm losing it.

And there was one thing that bothered me for a second: what if Sonja is still possessed by Mhaqal? And this is all a trick? I know it doesn't make any sense, it's just my paranoid brain talking. Right?

It must be fun for you guys to watch me go crazy, huh? Didn't anyone tell you it's a terrible thing to do to enable a sick person like myself? Do you get off reading my loony rants?

I Started Reading the Book

Posted by Kendra Temples on July 16th, 2018

It was only a matter of time before my curiosity got the better of me. The book starts with Steve waking up skinless in Hellworld with the goat that was supposed to be sacrificed that night at Eli's mansion. Just a normal goat, no human body or voice like in my vision. Some shayatin (plural for a shaytan, an evil jinn) are running off with Steve's fleshy husk, still in the shape of his body. He goes to attack them but is overpowered. Fortunately, the goat ripped Steve's head skin off the body before the shayatin took it away and gave it back to him. They trudged through the desert for awhile and got into scuffles and Steve helped the goat get a body to become Goat-Rob —that part was unnecessarily gross. Then they discovered a village. That's as far as I've gotten, the story hasn't caught up to my visions yet. I transcribed the most recent chapter for you guys below.

Journey to the Hellworld: Chapter 12

Steve plucked away at the stringy guts of a feline-like hell beast, strung across half of a de-thorned flesh-eating cactus bulb, while Goat-Rob struck a halved xylophonic ribcage of a bug-eyed serpent. The drive to find the monsters who stole our hero's skin had faded to a glimmer, and rested in the back of his weary mind. Life could go on, even without skin below the neck. He had a community now, a best friend, clothes, and a salve that protected his exposed muscles and ligaments from the wear of daily life. He found what could pass for an oasis in this world, a village of folk who struggled for survival, but still kept merriment, friendship, and stories alive. He could see himself growing old in this village, if growing old was even possible in the hell dimension.

And he built a life there, forgetting his

friends, his rock band, and his girlfriend who'd caused him nothing but trouble. He had a new band now, and even opened himself up to loving again, though the thought of exposing his disgusting body to another filled him with shame.

His new friend, a villager named Khassi, sang along in her eerily wet and low pitched voice. It was a discordant song that would have sounded demonic back on earth—a place where you could find the dulcet tones of a guitar, the pleasure of chocolate cake, the gentle warmth of a friendly sun, the caress of a cool breeze, and the intoxicating smell of a rose. But here it was nearly the only beauty that could be found. His band's songs were a ray of light in a dark unrelentingly hostile world. He'd never been in a band like this, one that brought such joy to listeners, one that made its audience enraptured and fall silent, one that gave him the friendship and gratitude of all who heard. It was a band that needed no clever name, or any name at all. It was the only band in existence in Hellworld. Our hero had essentially invented music.

Even in a place so cruel, he'd found something he'd never found on earth. He found a family who cared for him and valued him, gratitude for what little he had, and even a little patience from the countless hours he spent teaching Khassi how to turn her innately disgusting voice into song.

The whole village surrounded the three players in complete silence, a crowd of a small theater, enjoying a rare moment where they could forget their never-ending struggle to survive. But the hideous bellows of the three heads of a hydra-horse rang out from the village entrance, interrupting the peace and replacing it with a rapidly growing wave of panic.

Goat-Rob and Steve were whisked away out of sight into a hut, leaving their instruments behind. The two were fugitives, and all were at risk of peril if the shaytan King Delloq's collectors found them. The pair peered through dirty hides, that served as a door, to witness the disrupters.

"What's happening? Collection isn't for another two weeks," said Goat-Rob.

"This is bad," muttered Steve.

The roars of the hydra-horse grew louder as King Delloq's collectors trotted into the village square. The two shayatin riding the beast dismounted its long muscular boa-like torso to meet the village elder who handled such affairs. One was dog-faced, but with leathery, sagging and hairless mauve skin. It snorted as it breathed through its droopy elephant seal nose. The other looked nearly human, save for the impossible bulging muscles, until it lifted the visor of its smooth, bulb-like helmet, revealing crimson eyes and a long mouth that extended unnaturally down its neck.

The village elder cowered before them and pleaded. The collectors slowly drew their swords from their sides, silencing him and causing his wrinkled purple face to pale. The elder beckoned to another villager and relayed the collectors demands. The villager returned with a cart filled with a week's worth of hunting, foraging, and harvesting.

"We'll starve," said Steve.

Goat-Rob lay his hand on Steve's shoulder with a firm grip. "Better we starve than be ripped to pieces. The rest of us still have all of our skin, and we'd like to keep it."

"If we give them more now, they'll come back every week. We can't let them get away with this."

Goat-Rob tightened his grip and pulled

against Steve's forward lean. "Don't do anything stupid. It's out of our control."

Steve pulled his anger back inside, letting it boil within his skull, and watched the shayatin attach the cart to their steed. The collectors were about to leave, until they noticed the instruments left behind. They were meant to be hidden. Steve's band was the village's secret, a precious jewel that would surely be taken by King Delloq if the jinn knew of its presence. The collectors picked the sacred objects up and inspected them, turning them around and looking at them from every angle, trying to figure out what they could be. They turned to the village elder and the slight scrunching of his face betrayed their value. The collectors laughed as they smashed the instruments on the ground and stomped them to pieces.

Goat-Rob tackled Steve and stopped him from bursting out of the hut, but failed to prevent a commotion. The shaytan with the bulging eyes snapped to the direction of our hero's hiding place. He grunted and stomped over. Steve started for his sword but Goat-Rob swatted his arm before he could reach it. "Just shut up and let me handle this."

The goat-man got on his hands and knees

and stuck his head out of the opening in the cloth, hiding his humanoid body. Steve held his breath, cursing his temper, as Goat-Rob bleated cheerfully beyond the covering, involuntarily wiggling his butt. After a few endless moments, he backed out into a crouch and turned to Steve. “They’re gone. You’re lucky I’m adorable.”

I'm Not Crazy

Posted by Kendra Temples on July 20th, 2018

Maybe I'm muttering to myself in public, maybe I've been skipping showers, maybe I've been forgetful and spacey, maybe I've been overreacting to every little thing, and maybe I'm barely sleeping and having Sonja-level night terrors—but I'm not crazy. Not yet, anyways.

I'll admit it, you guys, this book is getting to me. I just can't make sense of it—it's hard to believe it even exists. So, some guy from the 70s had a vision of the future with a hero in an alternate dimension, and it happens to be about my ex-boyfriend?

And this other dimension, is it the invisible world of the jinn I've read about? Is some of the world pleasant, and Steve is just stuck in the hellish realm that's ruled by shayatin? Or is it another dimension all together that jinn also happen to live in? And I've never heard of a jinn named King Delloq. Is it because he's a minor monarch? Or a new one?

Why can't I find anything about the author online or any other books they wrote? How come this H.Q. Alma didn't finish the series? Did something happen to them, or did they just stop having the visions?

It's like a train wreck, I can't look away, but reading it and reliving Steve's suffering and the trauma of that night is definitely messing with my already warped pea brain. One of the reasons I love reading horror is that I can be scared, but I know I'm safe because it's not real. But this *is* real. I mean, I think it's real. The whole thing is bonkers.

And the people around me are starting to notice my deteriorating mental state too. Carlos is even more worried about me than usual. I can tell by his facial expressions and the increasing amount of treats he brings over.

Even Crash, in all of his own spacey-ness, is

noticing I'm acting weird. He told me, "Don't end up like the girl who worked here before you. She freaked out and bailed suddenly. We were just lucky you showed up, before I even had a chance to put up an ad."

I didn't bother telling him that I DID see a Craigslist ad for the job. He probably didn't know about it, or forgot or something—like I said, he's in his own world. I'm sitting next to him right now, behind the counter at work, and he's blasting music on his headphones—sounds like some shroomed-out trance—with his eyes closed, and he's hitting the counter with two promotional Float Void pens like he's drumming on stage in front of an adoring audience of stoned hippy chicks. Those pens will probably leak in a customers pocket! Show some respect for writing utensils, man!

A customer just came in, so I have to wrap this post up. I'll work up the courage to read the next chapter of the Hellworld book and transcribe it for you guys. I wouldn't want to let you down! Totally-not-crazy Kendra: out.

I Went to Disneyland!

Posted by Kendra Temples on July 22nd, 2018

Carlos surprised me with a trip to Disneyland yesterday! I wanted to go my whole life, but my mom would never take me. We could never afford family vacations—let alone to an expensive theme park in L.A. or Florida. My cousin Shelley and I would always talk about planning a trip there with her daughter Cindee, but we both knew we'd never be able to go. And then when I finally moved to L.A. and practically became neighbors with Pluto, Steve said it was a "dumb place for kids" and wouldn't take me.

Well, Carlos took me and it was awesome! I

wore Maleficent horns as we rode rides, ate Dole Whip by the light of tiki torches, smooched under fireworks, and was dazzled by the Electric Light Parade. I've never had someone take me on such a thoughtful and romantic date before, and the sex that night was incredible (I'm not going to lie—I left the horns on).

Driving through the cartoon hell in Mr. Toad's wild ride was so much better than the hell I visited in the floatation tank, and the haunted mansion was AMAZING! Even better than I imagined. The horrors were funny and friendly, and no one died for real. I skipped the Indiana Jones ride though. You know, the whole "Snakes. Why did it have to be snakes?" thing.

It felt so good to put behind Hellworld, like I could finally breathe, like my mind was clear for the first time in longer than I can remember. In the morning Carlos made me breakfast (Mickey Mouse pancakes with a bacon smile!) and I began working on a new short story. I can't remember the last time I wrote something other than this stupid blog. After he left, I threw *Journey to the Hellworld* in the trash. I know I just have a couple chapters left (I'd been saving it because I guess I didn't want the torture to end), but I need to put this all behind me. I don't even care if it's real anymore.

Journey to the Hellworld: Chapter 14

Posted by Kendra Temples on July 23rd, 2018

Okay, so I picked the book up again. I know, I know. I'm an idiot, but did you really think I was going to throw it away and pretend all of this never happened? And abandon Steve? Anyways, I had a moment to transcribe another chapter for you guys. Enjoy, I guess.

Journey to the Hellworld: Chapter 14

The hideous jinn's protruding eyeballs did not close, even as it appeared to sleep. Perhaps it had no eyelids, and this made Steve and Goat-Rob's ambush more complicated than expected. Steve suppressed his frustrated sighs as he crouched with Goat-Rob behind a chunk of decimated wall, the only remnants left of a settlement that had long since been destroyed. "Doesn't he ever sleep?"

"I think he *is* sleeping. And if not, I can't blame him with the way his friend floppy-face snores."

"Either way," said Steve, drawing his sword, "I can't wait any longer."

"Okay. I'll take spooky eyes, that beast will be no match for my legendary strength, and you take floppy-face—he's more your size."

"If it wasn't for me, you'd still be walking around on four legs with a scrawny little goat body."

"And if it wasn't for me, you wouldn't even have a face. Enough arguing."

The two stalked into the shayatin's camp until they stood over the sleeping collectors. They held their swords downward with two hands, ready to plunge them into the shayatin's necks. Steve glanced over at the goat-man, catching his eye to give the signal.

"Intruders! Intruders!" squawked a bird-thing perched on the wagon that the collectors took.

Goat-Rob plunged his sword into the red bodied shaytan as it began to sit up, missing its neck but planting the blade deep into its chest, causing its huge grotesque mouth to fill with dark purple fluid and its muscular arms to flail.

The other shaytan was quick and seized on Steve's surprise, slapping away his sword and leaping on to him, digging its claws into his back and clamping on like a tick. Steve stepped back and forth, teetering with the new weight, trying to keep his balance. "Help!"

Goat-Rob frantically pulled on his sword that stubbornly remained in the humanoid shaytan's corpse. "My sword! It's stuck!"

"Use your legendary strength, you freak!"

After another tug, Goat-Rob remembered that Steve's sword was laying close by and scooped it up. He quickly removed the wiry demon from Steve with a swift slice, and hacked the thing to bits, well beyond what was necessary. The shaytan's blood splattered onto the goat-man's face and horns as the many heads of the hydra-horse wailed. The bird-thing shrieked, "Murder! Murder! Murder! Murder!"

Steve was stunned by his partner's uncharacteristic savagery and forgot about the winged tattle-tale before it took flight. It soared towards King Delloq's castle. Our heroes looked on, unmoving, as the creature flew away and disappeared into the silent night sky.

"I wonder how many words that thing knows. Do you think it'll be a problem?" said Steve.

Goat-Rob muttered. "I don't know."

Steve walked over to the shaytan with the bulging eyes, that were now rotated in opposite directions and glazed over, and put a boot on its chest before he pulled out the sword. He smiled and snapped his head toward Goat-Rob. "Ha! Who's strong now?"

The goat-man didn't turn to face him, and instead walked over to the wagon to inspect the collector's spoils.

"What's the matter?" said Steve, "Aren't you going to tell me that you loosened it up for me?"

"You didn't have to call me a freak..."

"Christ, Rob. When did you get so sensitive?"

"We should head back to the village, now. We need to get them this food as soon as we can."

"You're right. I hope the elder isn't too angry about us going after the collectors. But he couldn't stay mad at his most beloved villagers too long, right Goaty?"

"Sure."

The morning after next they reached the village. As they approached they saw smoke coming from the village square. It was too much smoke for a cooking fire. And far too quiet.

The homes and workshops were destroyed, now smoldering ruins, and in the village square was a pile of flayed bodies. The only survivor was Khassi, left skinless but alive just long enough to tell Goat-Rob and Steve the horrors that King Delloq's minions wrought. And as she died, our heroes tearfully promised vengeance.

The Book Ended and I Think He's in Trouble

Posted by Kendra Temples on July 25th, 2018

I just finished the book. It caught up to my visions and ended on a cliffhanger. Delloq's soldiers captured Steve and Goat-Rob to take them back to his castle. There was a prologue too. It only read, "This story is of a world not so distant from ours, that awaits beyond a tender veil. And the thin curtain will be lifted by a reader, thirty nine years from its publication, who shall continue the story.

- H.Q. Alma"

He—or she—really was psychic, and the final passage was happening as I read it! I need to go to Steve immediately, before it's too late. I still haven't been able to project into Hellworld... I guess I'll have to take somewhat drastic measures.

Crash just replied to my text and said I could come over and buy some of his LSD. So yea, I'm about to take acid and visit a hell dimension. Sounds like a good time, right?

See you guys on the other side.

Hellworld on LSD

Posted by Kendra Temples on July 26th, 2018

Using tweezers, Crash ripped a little paper square off of the sheet of LSD. It was decorated with an image of Bart Simpson on a skateboard saying, “Don’t have a cow, man.” He put it in a cute little plastic baggy—like a sandwich bag for elves—and locked eyes with me as he handed it over. His usually glassy eyes defogged and became crystal-clear to impart the wisdom of an experienced tripper. “Kendra. Don’t have a cow… man.”

As soon as I was inside the float room, I put the square on my tongue. The magic chemicals dissolved in my mouth as I took a shower and hopped into the tank. I hit the water and was transported to Hellworld before I could close my eyes.

A massive castle dominated my view, composed of craggy purple towers jutting up into the dark red sky, like stalagmites made of moon rock. The sights, the sounds, and the smells were even more real than before. More real than reality. The world was breathing with me.

I heard desperate bleating, and turned around to see Steve and Goat-Rob. They had thick metal collars around their necks, attached together by a metal rod. The collars had loops around them, and each loop had a chain attached to it, and each chain was held by a different shaytan.

The creatures were uncanny amalgamations of human and animal, so grotesque that I would have felt sorry for them if they weren't torturing my boyfriend—I mean, ex-boyfriend. One had a dog's face, but hairless skeletal arms and hands and pointy horn-like ears, another had an enormous body, like a laughing buddha statue at a Chinese restaurant, but with huge veiny tits and a bull's head, and another looked like a seagull, but with large human eyes, a smooth melted ruby-colored skin and three human arms.

The shayatin surrounded Steve and Goat-Rob in a circle, walking them towards the castle, and sadistically tugged them in different directions—causing their victims to stumble and fall when yanked hard enough.

I started toward them and put my hands out to keep my balance. My hands flattened and separated slightly into blue and red tracers, like I was in an old 3D movie, and then snapped back to their regular fleshy form. I felt a warm electricity inside of me, and my body pulsed in sync with its separation.

I screamed. "Steve! Steve!"

Was I still just a projection? A pulse ran through my body. "Steve!"

The electricity dissolved and Steve's head raised just a little in my direction with a meek look of confusion. He didn't see me, but had he heard me? I wasn't sure, because when I screamed again he didn't react.

I followed the shayatin as they dragged Steve and Goat-Rob down into the dungeon of Delloq's craggy palace. They stripped them naked, exposing Steve skinless form and Goat-Rob's hairy humanoid body. I was a helpless spectator and started to regret my return to Hellworld.

Steve looked calm and his eyes scanned the musty dungeon, probably searching for exits. The smell of rotting flesh emanated from the body parts of various beings—angel wings, clawed paws, a fleshy tail (I hope it was a tail), pointy ears—all nailed against a board on the wall. A bin with wheels was filled with bones and feces. I remembered a book I'd read, it said bones and feces were food for some jinn, and I gagged. Hopeless wails from tortured souls echoed off the stone walls.

The dog-faced jinn grabbed Steve by the hair and pulled his face off. He screamed, "My face, give me back my face! Give me back my face!"

The screams escaped from his raw exposed skull, his jaw chattered as he spoke and I could see his tongue flapping around inside it. Without his lips his speech was impaired. His lidless eyes were glossy, full of panic and desperation. He grasped at his face held by the shaytan, who dangled it in front of him like a bully who stole a nerds comic book in a cheesy 80s movie.

"Give it back! Give it back!" Steve shouted.

The shaytan made an expression of mock

sadness and began to give Steve's drooping skin back before pulling it away and slipping it over his own head, like a Halloween mask. Steve's face distorted under the evil jinn's inhuman features. His snout stuck out between Steve's lips, and his ears caused the eyes to stretch into ovals, and the eyebrows to arch up towards the two points that looked like they'd nearly pierce through the top.

The jinn did a little dance and taunted him in his shaytan language—a demonic perversion of Arabic—until his comrades smacked him and carefully removed Steve's face to stow it away for Delloq's collection. They removed Steve's and Goat Rob's shackles, and pushed them into a hole in the stone floor. Steve and Goat-Rob yelped as their bodies hit the ground with a thud, and a grated door was closed on them. It must have been the cell for the worst offenders.

The three laughed and beamed from a job well done. I sniffled, tears filling my eyes. Then the melty smooth seagull jinn turned to me. It narrowed its gaze. Its two companions stopped and turned as well. They could see me. I looked at my hands. They were in retro-3D vision again. I was no longer a projection, I'd fully manifested in Hellworld!

My surprise and excitement was cut short when the ruby gull-creature screamed, and the three grabbed spears from a rack on the wall. I turned to run and tripped, falling on to my hands and knees. As I got up, I felt sharp blades run across my back, splitting my flesh. And the pain was real, so real. I tried to open my eyes, I tried to jolt the body I'd left behind into consciousness, but I blacked out. And the blackness burned.

I gasped and sucked in a mouthful of the humid air of our Float Void tanks. My back was on fire, as the salt water invaded the open bleeding wounds I'd brought back from Hellworld. I tried to shower and get the salt water out, knocking over half the room and getting blood on the white walls and decor. How is this possible? I thought I was safe in the tank—even if I did fully manifest in the hell dimension.

I was too messed up and confused to clean the room. I tried to take a Lyft home but couldn't figure out the app. All of the text was jumbled and gibberish.

I wandered in a random direction until I found myself in some sort of park and collapsed under a tree and I laid on the lawn staring at the sky through the branches. I would never find my way home, I was going to bleed out on this lawn. I took out my phone and called Crash, sob-blabbering. "I HAD A COW MAN. I HAD A FREAKING COW, OKAY CRASH?"

"Who is this?"

I dropped the phone and flattened. Eventually my eyes closed, and I got a little sleep before a sprinkler sprayed me awake. It turns out that the "park" I thought I was in was someone's dog pee soaked front yard. At least I was lucid enough to manage getting a Lyft back to my apartment.

Carlos was sitting on the ground in front of my door with his head in his hands. He looked up, probably from smelling my blood and dog piss soaked clothes, and jumped to his feet to give me a hug. "I've been so worried about you. I've been calling and texting. What happened to you? You're bleeding!"

He helped me inside and into the shower before he cleaned my wounds and somehow found a clean set of pajamas to wear. I showed him the book and told him everything. I mean everything: working at the library in the mansion, my boss's jinn-possessed wife, my boyfriend's skin being ripped off and transported to a hell dimension, and my current obsession with reading a book by a psychic author and traveling to said hell dimension in order to save Steve, because it was all my fault.

I thought he would think I was crazy or be mad about me obsessing over an ex-boyfriend, but he just gave me a hug and got into bed with me, and held me all night.

This morning he made me breakfast. He said he'd research H.Q. Alma, and took the book with him to see if he could find any clues. I can barely believe how cool he's being about it.

And Crash went to Float Void after I called, I guess he eventually figured out it was me screaming at him through the phone, and decided to make sure I was okay. He saved my ass—and my job—by cleaning up the huge bloody mess I made. Why are people so nice to me? I don't deserve it.

Get a Clue?

Posted by Kendra Temples on July 29th, 2018

I can't float right now, the cuts on my back still haven't healed. But at least I have proof that this is all real. Unless I gained some sort of Yogi-like flexibility and scratched my own back to shreds. It was my day off, so I went back to Eli's mansion to do some investigating about the book. My first reaction is revulsion when it comes even thinking about the library and mansion, but what else was I going to do? I'm incapable of doing normal human things—like going to the beach or the movies. Is that what normal people do?

I asked Andrea some questions and poked

around the collection to see if I could find any other books written by the author.

And... I came up with jack crap. Nothing. Who the hell are you H.Q. Alma?!?

But I did get to know Andrea better, and it turns out she's actually really cool! We have a lot in common—kind of a creepy amount. We like the same books and movies, are into supernatural stuff and other dimensions, we have a similar style (though hers is a bit bubblegum) and we even have the same favorite drink. She's like my evil twin. On second thought, I'm probably the evil twin.

You can tell when you're talking to her that she's really listening, not judging or thinking of the next thing to say. I felt so comfortable with her. Maybe a little too comfortable, because I opened up about my weirdo past—and freaky present.

I didn't tell her exactly everything, but I told her about my time working at the library and that my boyfriend died in the basement when we interrupted an exorcism. I kept it purposely vague because I didn't want her to feel unsafe in the library. I told her about my floating obsession too. I fibbed a bit and said that I was using the tank to induce lucid dreaming so that

I could talk to an imagined version of my dead ex-boyfriend. She said she liked to float and is interested in lucid dreaming too!

And I found out how interested she was when I ran into Sonja on the way out, wet haired and wearing only a terry cloth robe, while she ate avocado toast in the kitchen. She had the same blissed-out look on her face that our customers do when they come out of their float session. It turns out that Andrea recommended that she and Eli install a float tank at the mansion to help with the back pain she's been experiencing from her pregnancy.

One day, I too will be rich, and will be able to eat avocado toast in a $300 robe after coming out of my custom-made float tank that I've installed in my gothic mansion. Just buy my books (if I ever finish any of them) and make my dreams come true!

I didn't mention my LSD adventure or my shredded back. She looked so relaxed—and I didn't want to kill her buzz.

Guys. I just got a text from Carlos while I was writing this post. He said to come over to his house tonight. He found something out about the author of *Journey to the Hellworld* that he wants to show me! I'll keep you guys updated.

The Worst Reunion

Posted by Kendra Temples on July 30th, 2018

I arrived at Carlos' home. Usually it's lively: lights beaming out from under colorful shades, Telemundo blaring, kids playing, the smell of Mexican food cooking, and hugs from his Mom —who loves me for reasons I'll never know or understand. But instead it was dark and silent, like it was abandoned, like all of the "home" had been drained out, only leaving a husk of a house behind. I knocked on the door and Carlos answered, looking like a nervous puppy who knew he'd done something wrong. I went to give him a kiss, and I barely got a peck in return. I lowered my head to try and meet his averted eyes. "What's going on with you? Where is everyone?"

"Just come in."

I followed him, assuming we were going to his room, but we stopped in the living room. Sitting on the couch was my mother and my cousin (and former best friend) Shelley.

I hadn't seen them in years... not since I wrecked my old life and left town. I closed my mouth and swallowed. "What are you doing here? How did you even get here?"

"We drove," Shelly said with a smile as she handed me a cheap can of beer, the kind we'd drink together.

I took the beer. "All the way from Ohio?"

Shelley nodded slowly as if her head were heavy. She had dark circles under her eyes. They must have driven non-stop for the last few days.

"Kendra, sit down," said my mom.

I guess even after coming all this way, she wasn't on a hugging level with me yet. She took a deep breath, gripping and fiddling with her purse. I sat down. On the coffee table was the book, *Journey to the Hellworld*. This wasn't a reunion. It was an intervention.

"Carlos reached out to us on Facebook and

told us everything that's been going on with you. The drugs. The self harm. How you're obsessed with this blasphemous book, and making up nonsensical stories that you believe are true. Again!"

"Mom it's-"

"Let me speak. This place, this ungodly city, and your sinful writing—they're making you crazy. Come home, for at least as long as it takes to get your head right. You can move back into your old room. You can even have your computer privileges back, if you promise to use them to only write nice stories."

Apparently, two years later, I'm still technically grounded. Before I could tell her that I'm an adult with my own computer and will write what I please, Shelley chimed in with a hopeful smile in her eyes. "We can get drunk by the lake, like old times."

I looked down at my unopened beer, my fingers white from gripping it. I thought I'd never see them again after what I did. As soon as I jumped out of the cab of that stranger's 18 wheeler and set my dirty black Converse on the hot asphalt of L.A., I vowed to put my old life behind me. But you can't just edit out chapters of your life like you're writing a book, no matter how much you want to.

Carlos spoke up from behind me. "You should go. I think getting out of the city and away from your weird rich friends will be good for you. Of course I'll miss you, but I want what's the best for you, too. Going back home might be just what you need. I'll try and visit as much as I can."

"You won't visit," I said, "And L.A. is my home."

I looked away, and my eyes met the book. It had an envelope in it. Carlos must have noticed my glance. "I did find something about the author of that book. It's small, but maybe it's a clue. I wrote it down and put it in that envelope."

I started for the book but stopped at the feeling of his hand on my shoulder. The gentle firmness of his grip displayed a resolve that was uncharacteristic of him. "Stop. If you open that envelope, and walk out of here with that book-"

"You'll lose all of us!" My mom blurted out.

"It's us or whatever the hell that is," said Shelley, "C'mon cuz. We could be besties again. Don't tell me the fake avocado-toast-eaters you hang out with here are more fun than your cousin Shelley."

I hesitated long enough for my mom to burst into tears.

Shelley sighed. "Come on out, Cindee."

A little girl came out from the hallway. Cindee, my little cousin. They really brought her. "Aunty Kendra? Please come home."

So this was their secret weapon. She walked over to me, climbed on the easy chair and gave me a big hug. "I've missed you, Aunty Kendra."

I returned her embrace. "You crazy little monkey. You've gotten too tall, you're going to tip this chair over."

"Come home with us, Kendra," said my mom.

My head swam. What would a life back in Nowheresville, Ohio even look like? What would I do? How could have anyone back home really forgiven me? I struggled to picture a life for myself there, treated like a child at my mom's house, going to church, writing "nice" stories—whatever the heck those are.

I belong here, and Steve needs my help. And if there was a clue in that envelope that could help him...

I helped Cindee off of the love seat and stood up. My mom got up and embraced me. "So you are coming home!"

I broke out of her embrace. "No Mom, I'm not"

I walked out with that book and left her crying in my wake. She's the one who kicked me out of the house, anyway. She doesn't really want me—not the real me—just like my biological mom.

And Shelley, maybe she was my best friend once, but I've changed. I can find a new friend. And Cindee... I guess it was crappy of me to run out on her. She's had enough of that in her life.

And Carlos, well, that fucking "clue" turned out to be a break up letter. So he betrayed me too. I've been wanting to dump him anyways.

Just because I'm out of clues doesn't mean I'm going to give up on Steve. He never gave up on me. Well, I guess he technically did dump me too—but you know what I mean.

I think my wounds are healed enough to float again. I was worried it wouldn't be safe to go back to Hellworld, but I was texting with Andrea and she said she could make a protective charm for me. I didn't tell her everything. I just told her my lucid dreaming in the tank was starting to get really intense, and I was afraid I'd lose control.

She told me to text her before I go into the tank too, so that she could say a prayer for me and make the charm even stronger. She's so sweet. Who knows if it'll work, but I'm not going to turn the help down after what happened last time.

August

A Deal with a Devil (sort of)

Posted by Kendra Temples on August 2nd, 2018

I put on the charm necklace Andrea gave me. It was an old locket, inside was a colored pencil picture of an eye with a purple swirl for an iris. I sent her a thank you text before I got in the tank, and said the prayer she gave me too. I laid down in the water and closed my eyes, putting myself into the trance state.

I opened my eyes in Hellworld and I was in some sort of amphitheater, sitting among a court of shayatin and other jinn, I was even next to an angel! It was so freaking cool to see so many creatures beyond my imagination all at once. I looked at my hands and they looked normal, no blue and red tracers. But I had to check to see if I was a projection or manifestation. I turned to the angel and tried to think of something to say. “So uh... do you know Gabriel or Michael?”

I immediately cringed and said to myself, “Do you really think that all angels know each other, Kendra?”

The angel didn’t reply, and I wasn’t sure if it was because I was so awkward or if they couldn’t hear me. I yelled this time, to make sure, “So are you on break right now? Or uhh, doing an errand for the big guy?”

Not my finest moment, but do you have a better angel icebreaker? It didn’t matter though, they couldn’t see or hear me. I was a wandering spirit, a witness with no influence in this dimension. I was both relieved and disappointed. I couldn’t help Steve, but I was safe.

The deep booming of drums filled the amphitheater and the audience cheered in a cacophony of supernatural voices. At first I was excited to see what the show was, but my excitement quickly turned to dread when I saw my skinless and naked ex-boyfriend Steve on his knees in front of King Delloq in the middle of the amphitheater stage. He had a plump jinn with round glasses and blood-red skin standing next to him. The red jinn didn't seem like a jailer or guard. His posture was sympathetic toward Steve and they were discussing something.

The king sat behind a ridiculously high podium and looked down at them from a stool with legs that matched the podium's height. He was wearing Steve's skin, with his white cat-like head popping out of the shredded neckline, so small for his body, and his ears and nose were longer and pointier than a typical feline. He didn't look anything like I'd imagined, he was almost sort of cute, yet his pure evil still shone out and gave him a commanding presence. Standing next to the podium was a jinn with long spindly legs, a smug look, and a powdered wig.

It didn't take me long to figure it out: this was a trial. It was one of the jinn trials I'd read about in occult books.

King Delloq slammed a gavel on the podium and with only one hit the entire audience went dead silent, except a baby jinn which began to cry. Delloq yelled something in a language I couldn't understand and the guards took the baby away—probably to some sort of tiny baby prison or torture chamber. Imagining all the cute baby-sized torture devices and the ridiculousness of it gave me a smile, until I realized they probably *did* have baby-sized torture devices in this dimension. This was real.

Delloq leaned his body over the podium and pointed his gavel at Steve with a triple jointed arm that stretched the human skin above it unnaturally. His voice boomed, speaking in his shaytan language, and it widely varied in pitch from the lowest baritone to the highest glass-breaking screech.

The jinn, who I assumed was Steve's lawyer, translated for him, then Steve yelled with his lipless mouth, "What do you mean I stole a face? That face was mine. Mine! Just because you found it... You can't play finders keepers with someone else's face!"

His lawyer translated to the king, and it sounded like he was also pleading Steve's case.

Delloq laughed and clicked his tongue. The guards wheeled out a shaytan with stumps for arms and legs. The crowd gasped and murmured. The legless, armless shaytan stretched his neck out toward Steve, pointing with his only movable appendage. He screeched and wailed, at times crying like a baby in his testimony. Delloq looked on with a satisfied smile, his head lazily propped up by his hand and elbow on the podium. After what felt like forever, he turned to Steve's lawyer and said one word, like he was saying "See?"

Steve lowered his head and clenched his fists, "You would have done the same."

Delloq banged his gavel and the guards took him away. He didn't struggle, he just walked with them, his head hanging low.

The crowd hooted and hollered, chattering in a disgusting display of pleasure. As I looked around the crowd in horror, I noticed one of the jinn was turned in their seat toward me. Its red eyes were staring right into mine. I looked behind me—this was impossible. I was only a projection, no other being in this world could see me.

The jinn was clearly a shaytan, though it was humanoid and strangely beautiful. It wore a widow's peak crown of silver scales, and there was what looked like dramatic theatrical eye makeup with exaggerated wings painted on its pale green skin. It nodded at me and smiled, revealing its long fangs. I froze. It was Mhaqal.

Mhaqal stood up and walked toward me. I ran down the amphitheater stairs, nearly tripping toward the exit. Before I turned down the hall I saw Goat-Rob ram into Delloq's podium, causing it to sway and the king to steady himself so he wouldn't fall.

I charged past the exit and found myself facing Mhaqal. She stood with her legs firmly planted in the ground. "Kendra, Kendra. I don't want to hurt you. And I can't even if I wanted to, I am but a spirit here, a witness like you. I merely want to talk."

I froze. I don't know if she put me in a trance or if I was just too scared to move. Either way there was no escaping her. "What do you want?"

"I want to return home. I am trapped in your world. Kept inside the one you call Andrea."

"Andrea? What you mean? Have you possessed Andrea?"

"Andrea is from an ancient lineage of Keepers. She has the ability to trap demons, jinn, and other spirits inside her. She jails them in her body and soul to protect the outside world from their influence."

"But why would she put herself so close to Sonja? Isn't she putting her at risk?"

"The occult library, of course. The books have not been destroyed, merely moved to the basement. She seems to be looking for a way to rid the world of me once and for all. Clearly, she knows me not well," Mhaqal said, revealing her fangs again in a twisted smile.

The basement. Great. My favorite place in the mansion to go to to trigger my PTSD.

"I need your help, little Kendra," said Mhaqal, "I need you to free me from Andrea. An exorcism of sorts."

"Why would I do that? You ripped off Steve's skin and condemned him to Hellworld! You fucking traumatized me for life!"

"Ah, yes. I've always had a bit of a temper. Do you think I like constantly being summoned by foolish humans and trapped in their disgusting bodies? My life isn't all fun and games and tormenting. I just want my freedom. I want to go home. I'm sick of your world."

"And why should I help you after everything you've done to me?"

"Because if you release me from Andrea, I can return to this realm, not as a ghost, but as a resident, and I can help Steve. I can get his skin back. I can save him from an eternity of torture. And I'll leave you and him alone forever."

All this time I just wanted to help Steve. Was this really my only option?

"Think on it," she said, "Merely remove her necklace. Like you did with Sonja." She gave me a wicked smile and then I woke up.

"Merely" take off her necklace, eh? That didn't go so well last time. All I have to do is unleash an evil jinn into the world, and Steve is saved. But I can't do that, right? Even I'm not that stupid. I mean, what if it's a trick? I've never heard of a "Keeper," in all my occult research. Releasing Mhaqal is such a terrible idea—there's no way I should do it. Right?

Steve

Posted by Kendra Temples on August 3rd, 2018

I can't stop imagining all of the horrible things that Delloq's minions are doing to Steve. I've got no reason to trust Mhaqal, but I can't give up on him, and I don't know how to help him otherwise. And what would I do with myself if I gave up? Beg Carlos to take me back, and pretend none of this ever happened?

Visiting this hell dimension is my life. I have no friends, no boyfriend, no family... only Steve.

I'm Such an Idiot

Posted by Kendra Temples on August 5th, 2018

It was too late to turn back now. I had to save Steve from King Delloq and help him get his skin back. It was the only way.

The huge cross necklace Andrea wore around her neck was held tight with a thick chain—the kind you need a saw or bolt clippers to get off. So I went to the hardware store and bought a hacksaw I could fit in my oversized purse. And as luck would have it, Andrea invited me over to the library. She said she had something important to show me.

When I got to the mansion, Andrea greeted me with a warm hug and smile. She's so nice, it made it even harder to break her trust—and her sacred vow of keeping an evil spirit inside her to protect humanity.

"I can't wait to show you what I found," she said.

"Where are Sonja and Eli?" I asked, as I followed her to the library.

"Sonja's with her doula and Eli is still 'down undah' shooting a movie about a wallaby that saves St. Patrick's Day."

I was too nervous to comprehend the ridiculous premise of Eli's movie—the tension was killing me. As soon as she got into the library, I closed the door behind us, took out the hacksaw and pounced on Andrea's back, knocking her down. I sat on her back and pushed her head to the ground as I began to steady my hacksaw. She was totally pinned. I guess depression induced weight gain is good for something.

"What the fuck are you doing? Get off of me," she said after an exasperated cry.

I apologized profusely (and probably unintelligibly) as I sawed at the chain pressed against the back of her neck. She struggled and grunted under my weight. "You don't know what you're doing! You have to stop!"

"I can't," I said through clenched teeth.

Cutting through the chain was taking too long. I'd barely made progress on one side of the link because the force of my sawing was jiggling it. So, I took my hand off her head and slid my fingers under the already tight chain and pulled it back to steady the link.

Andrea shook and made choking noises but I didn't stop. I couldn't—I was finally making progress. And it's not like I was going to kill her. Plus I think she was mostly faking it.

I guess her adrenaline must've kicked in because she finally mustered enough strength to buck me off of her, causing my hacksaw to slip and cut a gash in her shoulder.

She ran to the back of the room and pulled something out of her desk. She spun around with a large sacrificial knife in hand and fury in her eyes. "I don't know what you think you're doing Kendra, but it's not going to happen. I come from a sacred order of Keepers, pledged to protect the world from evil spirits. And I will stop at nothing to-"

Her speech was cut short when the huge book I threw into her temple knocked her out. I'll spare you the obvious pun and my pathetic rationalizations.

I flipped her over onto her back and into our original position. She was muttering and semiconscious, but still. It was much easier to saw through her necklace without her wriggling. Just as I was about to finish sawing the other side of the link, I realized Sonja was standing right next to me. “Kendra! What the hell are you doing?"

She went to grab my shoulder but I slapped her hand away. I was seconds away from removing that necklace, and saving Steve from eternal suffering.

The link finally snapped. I yanked at the chain, causing it, and the large metal cross attached to it, to slide across the room. The shelves around me shook, creating waterfalls of books. The windows and walls trembled until the shaking became so violent that it shattered the glass. Mhaqal was free.

I looked over to Sonja, she was sobbing and quivering. "What have you done? Why?"

I didn't stick around to answer, I bolted out the door to my car and drove off.

Sonja's been furiously texting me today. She wants to know what I did. And I guess Andrea suffered a fairly major concussion and is in the hospital. She said I could've killed her. Turns out knocking someone out cold isn't like the movies where they just wake up with a headache the next day.

I hope she's okay. I've been avoiding my phone so I don't know. We could have been friends, and I do this. Typical.

I hope she doesn't press charges—at least until I've had a chance to free Steve from the Hellworld prison.

Once a Tormentor, Always a Tormentor

Posted by Kendra Temples on August 7th, 2018

I put myself into a trance in the floatation tank and woke up standing in a torch-lit tunnel, deep in the dungeons of King Delloq's palace. I walked down the hall hoping to find Mhaqal, so we could get Steve out of here. I heard her distinct cackle coming from a chamber and held my breath as I stepped in.

It was her. She was standing next to Steve who was in a tall human size birdcage with his arms tied back. And next to the cage was Goat-Rob's severed head on a pike. Poor sweet Goat-Rob.

The cage that held Steve was lined with spikes pointing inward, ready to pierce his exposed twitching muscles. Mhaqal had her hand in the cage, stroking Steve skinless face with the long sharp nail of her index finger. "You remember me, don't you?" she said, letting her snake like tongue flick in and out of her mouth.

She turned to me, already aware of my presence. “How timely of you to arrive now, little Kendra.”

Steve looked around frantically, but restrained by the threat of being impaled by the spikes, "Kendra? You mean... My Kendra? She’s here? How...”

"Steve!" I yelled, but he couldn't hear me.

"Yes, my sweet, you can't see her, you can't hear her, but your Kendra is here watching you," said Mhaqal.

Steve quieted his body, "I... I don't believe you. This is all part of the torture."

"She's here," said Mhaqal, “And she's the reason I'm here. She was foolish enough to free me again, thinking I would help you get your skin back. But I just couldn't resist torturing you further. Besides, it's my job. I'm King Delloq's head tormentor after all."

Steve's lidless eyes began to well up with blood stained tears until they drizzled down his face and exposed jaw. "No... It can't be..."

Mhaqal picked up a bucket next to her and looked at me with a smile before dumping the contents over the cage, letting the hundreds of fire ants inside crawl on to Steve's body.

"Oh, but it is," Mhaqal said as Steve squirmed, his body resisting the urge to cast off the insects.

I screamed and rushed to Steve, trying to brush off the ants in vain as Mhaqal laughed. I gave Steve a touch-less embrace before I willed myself back into our world. I couldn't watch him suffer any longer.

When I opened my eyes, I felt as hopeless as I did in Hellworld. There was nothing I could do to stop this. I sobbed and screamed as I showered, banging my fists against the wall.

And then my phone dinged. It was a text from Andrea. It read: "I forgive you."

Now my tears were accompanied by manic laughter. The whole thing was so absurd. How could someone be so nice? I sent her a "get well soon" GIF (a black cat with an ice pack and thermometer dancing) and immediately regretted it, thinking she would think I was making fun of her.

But she replied with "LMAO" and sent a GIF of her own, a super pixelated emoji with sunglasses that looked like it was from the nineties. It was pointing through the screen, and the bubble letters above it said, “It’s cool.”

"How can you forgive an idiot like me?" I replied.

Andrea: I don't hold grudges. And, I need your help. We have to stop Mhaqal and clean up this mess

Andrea: Will you help me?

Me: Yes. Just tell me what you need me to do

Andrea: Meet me at the mansion. 12pm. We'll put a stop to this

Andrea: Once and for all.

The Final Visit

Posted by Kendra Temples on August 9th, 2018

I met up with Andrea at the mansion and she snuck me into the float room. And guess where they decided to install the tank? Yep. The basement. In the room that the ritual to exorcise Mhaqal took place. It wouldn't be *my* first choice to put a supposedly relaxing room in the mansion, but I guess Sonja was blacked out that night and doesn't have the same associations that I do. So I was terrified, shaking, and having flashbacks—but I had to be strong for Steve.

Once we got inside the room, things got real weird, real fast. Andrea laid out all these ritualistic items; candles, ornate knives, salt, sage, potions—even blessed aerosol sprays.

"This is a protectant spray," she said holding up a can that looked like a hairspray can, but had a cartoon demon on it and the label "Evil Spirit Barrier—Caution: Flammable!"

"Please, undress. I need to cover your entire body," she said as she shook the can.

"You mean naked?" I asked, "Are you serious?"

"Yes," she said with a stony face.

"Aren't you going to buy me dinner first?" I said.

Andrea wasn't amused. "I need you to take this seriously Kendra. Now strip."

I turned away and undressed. I'm not used to being naked around anyone other than people close to me. I was homeschooled, and didn't spend much time in locker rooms. I turned back around to Andrea with my arms folded, covering my breasts. "Okay, so I'm naked. What now?"

Andrea tugged my wrists to have me unfold my arms and gave the can another shake. "Close your eyes."

She sprayed me head to toe with the evil spirit protectant. It was sticky on my skin and even burned a little. It smelled like rotten meat and I coughed and gagged when it went up my nostrils after she sprayed me directly on my face.

"Sorry, I know this isn't pleasant but it works," said Andrea.

She took out a jar of salt and shook it out of the narrow opening, drawing a large circle of the crystals. "This will make sure you can return easily. We don't want you to get stuck in the dungeon in Hellworld."

After she finished the circle, she instructed me to lay down on it with my legs spread and palms up. She lit three large black candles, placing them inside the circle in a triangle shape.

Then she took out her knife.

"This is going to hurt a little," she said, putting her finger up before I could protest, "But it's absolutely necessary. It will give you the ability to not only manifest in Hellworld physically, you'll have the power to bind Mhaqal."

She crouched down and held my wrists, pinning my hand to the ground, holding the blade over my palm. "Sorry about this."

I screamed as she slowly carved an upside

down triangle on my palm. "Stop! Please!"

"You can do this, Kendra, " she yelled over my screams, “Think of Steve.”

She held down my other wrist, the hand I broke that night. I cried as she carved the second triangle, deeper than before. Through my tears and pain I saw her looking at me, giving me a warm smile. "You're doing great."

The wound on my hand throbbed and the pain traveled all the way up my arm and into my chest. It was hard to imagine why she was doing this, but I trusted her. And it was basically my last chance to help Steve.

She stood up and admired her handiwork. "Once you get to Hellworld you'll be happy I did this," she said, gazing into the crimson wetness of the blade like she was thinking of tasting it.

"Okay, one last thing," she said, as she turned off the light, filling the room with darkness except for the light from the candles. She burned the sage and walked around the room, leaving looming clouds of smoke.

She picked up one of the large candles and stood between my legs holding it with two hands. Incantations flowed from her mouth as the flickering candlelight cast dancing shadows across her face. "Seplitudious, b'have oshra. Dumbuldy lungus, tee damule."

She took a deep breath and let it hang in the air before continuing. "Abracadabra. Abracadabra!"

I laid there naked, thinking “What the hell is she doing?”

Abracadabra isn’t just something amateur magicians say at kids’ birthday parties, it’s actually one of the earliest magic incantations. But it sounded like a joke. I spoke up. "Are you —are you sure..."

She shushed me loudly and took another breath. "Ooga. Ooga booga. Ooga booga booga. Oooooooga boooooooog-"

“Are you kidding me?" I said trying to sit up without pressing my throbbing palms on to the floor.

She laughed. Not a chipmunk Andrea laugh, but a laugh I heard a long time ago, a laugh of two voices. A laugh of an evil jinn. My shock was broken by Andrea splashing hot wax on my body.

"You really are just so stupid, aren't you little Kendra?" said Andrea.

"M-Mhaqal?" I said.

"Yes, it's me. It's always been me. There's no such thing as a Keeper, you should know that from your studies. And you never freed me, I've been free this whole time, in complete control of this weak willed soul," Andrea said, her teeth and eyes now those of Mhaqal.

As I began to stand to run, Andrea—I mean Mhaqal—wrapped her hand around my neck, her fingernails growing into my flesh. She lifted me up by the neck with incredible strength. The walls of the room pulsed, revealing the hidden spells written all over them in Arabic, Hebrew, and a language I didn't recognize.

She shoved me through the open door of the flotation tank, slamming my head back against the slick wall. She crawled into the tank with me. Inside Andrea's skinny body, in the shadowed room, she looked like a spider creeping to its prey: me, stupid little Kendra.

She straddled me, and her weight pushed me down into the water—the salt entered the wounds in my hands and burned. Andrea-Mhaqal wrapped her hands around my neck again, tightening her grip. She dunked me, getting the salt into my eyes. When she lifted me out her red eyes locked into mine through my furious blinking as she said, "Why don't we visit Steve? He's being drawn and quartered today."

Mhaqal plunged my head into the water again, holding me under until I was so starved for breath I became lightheaded. And then I woke up in Hellworld. In the dungeon.

Steve was on a rack, his wrists and ankles tied by ropes attached to rollers with cranks. Mhaqal, in her original form—hairy legs, a snakes crown and long fangs and nails—stood next to the rack, staring at me. "So good of you to come, Kendra."

At hearing my name, Steve lifted his head to see me. He could see me! "Kendra? Is it really you?"

"Steve!" I yelled and rushed toward him, finally with the ability to embrace him. I didn't care how disgusting he looked. I just wanted to hold him.

But Mhaqal snapped her fingers and two shayatin materialized next to me, each grasping one of my arms to keep us apart.

"It's really her," said Mhaqal. "The reason for all of your suffering. The reason you're in hell."

Steve put his head back onto the rack and I could see blood tears dripping from his eyes.

"I'm here to save you! We can get out of this place and get your skin back!" I said struggling, trying to free myself from the grasp of the shayatin.

Steve sobbed. “I don't care about my skin! I just want this all to end!”

Mhaqal gave a snake smile. “Perhaps that can be arranged. I am not without mercy.”

She snapped her fingers again, and the dungeon fell silent. The sounds of clanging chains, shuffling of guards and screaming of prisoners disappeared, even the smell of blood and rot and urine went away. The grip of the shayatin became as still and as hard as stone. The dust of the dungeon hung in midair. Steve's pulsing body became still. Time had stopped except for Mhaqal and I.

Mhaqal waved her hand and the walls of the dungeon began to come apart, the stones separated and rotated away in perfect harmony without ever touching. The dirt behind the underground dungeon walls slid outward, the particles rolling away, until we were standing in a huge crater, underneath the pieces of the tower and its inhabitants. I saw a floating bathtub frozen in time with a jinn taking a bath in it. Above us, King Delloq spun away like a boomerang on his throne of bones.

The world continued to fall away, even the

redness of the sky was sucked into an abyss, until the three of us and the frozen guards holding me stood on an endless mirrored plane within a black void. Mhaqal somehow had the powers of a god here. But how? She wasn't even a high up jinn or demon, she was just a lowly shaytan.

"Did you create this hell for Steve?" I asked. "This isn't the real hell dimension, is it? It's a personalized planet size torture chamber just for Steve!"

Mhaqal smiled with a secret behind her lips. "Yes, this is a planet size torture chamber, just for Steve. But I didn't create it. You did."

I couldn't speak. I tried but my voice was caught in my throat.

“This world didn't exist until you imagined it in the tank and wrote about it in your pathetic blog-”

“Wait, you’ve been reading my blog?”

“Just because I’m thousands of years old doesn’t mean I can’t use the internet. I read how desperate you were to see Steve: so desperate that you’d rather see him in hell than never see him again. So I granted your wish by enchanting your float tank, giving you the power to snatch his soul from a peaceful oblivion, and place him into a world created from your anxieties. And you visited him again and again, subjecting him to torture born from your trauma."

"But the book..."

"My fabrication! I filled in the gaps you left. Steve's torture has been a beautiful collaboration between the two of us."

I didn't want to believe it, but it made so much sense. The snake monsters, the white cat shayatin, the insects, Steve skinless body. They were all of my anxieties and phobias. The landscape and creatures of this world, they were just like those old science-fiction fantasy books and movies from the 70s and 80s we bonded over when we first started dating online. The red sky and orange sand was just like the cover of Steve's copy of *Dune*. I was the creator of Steve's personal hell dimension.

"If I leave, and if you don't kill me when I wake up, and I never return, will Steve be free?" I asked Mhaqal.

"No. If you do that I will put this world back together and Steve will never leave this dungeon. He will be torn apart and his sentient remains will be tortured here for all of eternity."

I began to cry. "What do I do?"

Mhaqal snapped her fingers and Steve unfroze, his body wriggling and pulsing once again. She stuck her palm out and the shayatin holding me let go as they flew off into oblivion. An axe materialized at my feet.

"You have to kill him. You have to kill him again, and send his soul into nothingness," she said.

“I can’t!” I cried.

The ropes on the rack began to pull and tighten on their own, stretching Steve’s limbs.

Steve screamed and lifted his head to look me in the eyes. "Just kill me, Kendra. Please kill me, I can't take this any longer."

How could I kill him again? All I wanted was to see him, to visit him. I didn't want this. I didn’t want to lose him.

“You'd rather let him suffer for eternity, wouldn't you? I knew it!"

She was right. But I knew what had to be done, I picked up the axe and walked toward Steve on the rack, my sobs growing with each step. I stood next to Steve and his lidless eyes met mine. "Do it. Please."

I lifted the ax above my shoulders, positioning myself to chop his head off as cleanly as possible. My hands shook, and the ax quivered in the air and the wounds on my palms throbbed as I gripped it tightly. "I can't! I can't do this! I can't kill you again!"

Steve groaned and rolled his lidless eyes. "Kendra can you stop being a selfish bitch for two seconds and kill me already?"

It really was Steve. My sobs began to mix with laughter and I put the ax down. "I'm not going to kill you."

"Kendra!" said Steve.

Mhaqal cackled, reveling in my suffering. But she stopped when she saw I was smiling at her.

Steve wasn't some sort of tragic hero, he was just my barely lovable asshole ex. Obsessing over the moment of his death and imagining him as some sort of science-fiction fantasy hero trading quips with a magical animal friend in a hell dimension wasn't the story I wanted to tell myself about him anymore.

I looked at Steve and I let him go. I just let him go, like letting out a breath I'd forgot I was holding.

His skin began to reappear as he faded away with closed eyes and a peaceful smile.

“No!” Mhaqal screeched with infinite voices.

"We're doing this my way!"

She gestured to Steve before he'd completely disappeared and brought him back. Her flexed fingers pointed towards him, and with the control of a hundred tiny invisible clawed hands, she peeled off his new skin in small strips. She twisted her wrist and the rack began to tighten, stretching and elongating his limbs. Steve screamed in agony.

I lifted my hands, palms up, and began to shape the darkness. I had power here, perhaps even more than Mhaqal. I could do cool shit like waving my hands around to manipulate the world too. The darkness materialized into the skinless villagers, multiplying into an army bearing swords, spears, and shields. Leading them was Goat-Rob on Betsy, the giant hairless anteater. They stood in formation, trained on Mhaqal, waiting for my instruction.

Mhaqal smiled. "Are you sure you want to do this, little Kendra? Die here, and you'll never wake up. You'll suffer for eternity in a far worse place."

As she spoke, creatures emerged from the darkness behind her: the snake-eyed serpents, a flock of black chrome vultures, swarms of insects, and King Delloq riding a bellowing hydra-horse with an army of his grotesque minions behind him. Mhaqal's army became still with a clatter of their many blades, and silent except for the collective rising and falling of their breath. We were outnumbered.

I signaled for my army to charge and our enemies followed suit. The two sides rushed past us and collided like two waves in a storm. The mirrored floor made the battle nearly indiscernible. It was a kaleidoscope of steel, scales, sinewy muscle and the splattering of blood. The dancing display of struggle and suffering was accompanied by a symphony of creatures screaming and metal screeching. As hard as it was to make out any individual scene, I could tell that my side was being overpowered.

I ran toward the battle, creating yellow orbs of energy in my hands. I was useless with weapons, and I figured they were beneath a goddess like me anyway. I made my way through the battle, jumping over slain bodies, and ducking the swing of weapons while shooting beams from my hands, exploding monsters and minions into dust with a pop. Like a total bad-ass action hero. I'll admit I was sort of enjoying the moment. In our world, I would have fallen flat on my face with my first step.

In the chaos of battle I didn't see Mhaqal approach, wading through the bodies, alive and dead, as if they were overgrown grass. She was nearly ten feet away when I finally noticed her reflection in the ground. I charged up and shot a beam of energy her way as I blasted another into an advancing serpent, but she sprung into the air, over the energy beam and knocked me over. She slammed on to me with her body and her strong claws wrapped around my neck, closing my airway. With every lost breath I felt my power growing weaker, and my army began to lose its strength too. My eyes darted around, witnessing the villagers being overtaken and slaughtered by Delloq's minions.

The shayatin who no longer had enemies around them to fight, surrounded me and began to pull my hair, claw at my skin and clothes, and bite my flesh, as Mhaqal tightened her grip and gazed into my unfocused eyes, wearing her murderous smile. "How does it feel, little Kendra? How does it feel to be torn apart by your worst fears and anxieties?"

She was right. These were MY anxieties, not

hers. This was my world, not hers. The hands, claws, and teeth left my body, and Mhaqal's grip loosened as she was overtaken by her army—now under my control. The monsters and minions throughout the battlefield abandoned their fights and swarmed around Mhaqal. I watched, sitting from the floor and catching my breath as she reached out toward me from the enveloping pile of creatures. Her last look to me before she disappeared into them was not a look of fear. It was annoyance.

I walked away from the growing mass of jinn and beasts towards Steve. I kneeled down and lifted his hanging head towards mine and kissed his lipless mouth. His skin returned again and I held my kiss until he faded out of existence.

I took a moment to witness the wreckage of the battlefield before being jolted back into our world by screams and the feeling of my hands and eyes burning with salt.

"Where am I? Where am I?" Andrea screeched frantically, splashing water as she scrambled into the corner of the tank like a frightened cat.

I sat up and pushed the door open, letting in light, and she screamed even louder, "Who are you? Who are you? Why are you naked? Where the fuck am I?"

Mhaqal must've completely taken over Andrea, because she had no recollection of anything about the library or me. I'm not even sure if Andrea is her real name, she doesn't remember that either.

Poor Andrea, waking up with no memory in a dark room with a naked stranger who tells you that you've been possessed by a demon (let alone a jinn, which she's never heard of). It can't be a great way to start a week. I took her home and she's been staying with me. She doesn't have an ID and there are only three contacts in her phone. Me, Eli, and Sonja. Creepy. There were no social media apps or accounts on her phone to give clues either.

She had a surprising amount of games installed, though. I wonder how many hours of torture they saved me and Steve.

There was no trace of Andrea online. No missing persons reports, no social profiles, nothing. And I'm 99.999% sure that this isn't just Mhaqal acting and pretending she left Andrea's body. Mhaqal can lie and pretend, but she's not capable of empathy. I don't think she could understand depression, let alone portray it in the way Andrea is showing. Mhaqal must still be out there, as slippery as ever. At least I can rest knowing it's not my fault. This time.

I'll try and keep you updated about Andrea, but forgive me if I drop off the map—my hands are still fucked and I'm not getting much sleep. Between her night terrors and mine it's not exactly slumberland around here.

I texted Sonja to see if she could help, but I haven't heard back. I'd be surprised if I ever hear from her again. If I do, I'll let you guys know.

Missing Pieces

Posted by Kendra Temples on August 12th, 2018

I quit my job at the float spa. My boss was so relieved, I guess she'd been wanting to fire me for weeks but felt too bad to do it because I seemed like such a mess.

Andrea's memory hasn't returned yet and we still haven't figured out who she is, or her real name. We decided the name Andrea works. Her personality is completely different than when she was possessed by Mhaqal. She's really shy and quiet, and doesn't wear any makeup or fix her hair. I took her to Target and she bought some pretty lame clothes.

I'm not sure what to do with her, I don't want

to take her to the police and she doesn't want to go either. I guess she could live with me, other than having the temperament and taking up the space of a drunk kraken when she's in bed, she's not a terrible roomie. Plus it'll be nice to have some help with the rent now that I'm jobless. Is two jobless slobs sharing an apartment better than one? Jobless slobbery loves company, I guess.

Maybe she could go back to working at the library? Or maybe Eli could open up his big old checkbook and give her a pity bonus like he did for me.

Sonja hasn't texted back and I reached out to Carlos to see if he would consider getting back together with me, but I haven't heard from him either. Based on my social media sleuthing there's a good chance he's already started dating someone else.

Are you reading this, pink sweater? I'm not impressed that you beat Carlos at foosball at Too Far Bar last Saturday at 8:59pm and got 126 likes for it!

My family is a lost cause, but I hope he at least takes me back. He was such a good guy and I took him for granted. He was a real person too. A real not-dead person. I still think of Steve all the time of course. But I try to remember the happy memories of him, and even the memories of him being an asshole. I'm remembering him as a real person, not some sort of self-sacrificing tragic hero.

Don't get me wrong, I'm still messed up in the head. I'm thinking of seeing a therapist. I guess right now you guys are kinda like my therapist, huh?

Sonja Had Her Baby

Posted by Kendra Temples on August 16th, 2018

Eli called to let me know the good news. It's a girl. And you know what they named her? Kendra.

Just kidding, they named her after someone who isn't a total shit head. It was nice to hear Eli's voice, I guess he wasn't mad at me for attacking Andrea with the intention of releasing an evil spirit that had previously possessed his wife—probably because he heard it all secondhand and understands that I was being manipulated. And supposedly Sonja isn't mad anymore either, but she's just "not interested" in talking with or seeing me.

He said he'd transfer me some money for Andrea, whoever she is. I guess she'll be able to help with the rent after all.

I asked him if he had any documents from when he hired her, but he said hiring her was a spontaneous decision—he met her in a bookstore and got to talking—and he didn't do it through his lawyer like usual. Then he got real serious and asked, "So what happened to Mhaqal?"

"I'm not sure, last I saw she was covered in a pile of monsters and evil spirits in a hell dimension," I said, "But I doubt that was the end of her."

"So she still out there?"

"Probably. Comforting isn't it?"

"Stop being sarcastic. We're talking about the safety of my wife and child."

I apologized.

"I'm going to have to figure something out, look into professional help," he said.

After that ominous statement he said goodbye and hung up. I wonder what he meant by that? Was he going to hire some sort of supernatural bodyguard?

I've been wondering where Steve is since I released him from Hellworld. Maybe he's just gone. I guess I can be okay with that.

And I bought a pet python and named it Mrs. Friendly. Really. I'm hoping she'll help me with my fear of snakes. So far she's pretty much freaked me out every day and I've been having Andrea do most of the work of taking care of her. I let her slither around my shoulders once —until I had a panic attack. I've been getting used to her slowly, and I even fed her yesterday without hyperventilating.

Andrea is weirdly obsessed with her. There's a lot of weird things about the real Andrea. She sounds like she's praying in her sleep, and she has these geometric tattoos on her back that I've been trying to research—they actually kind of remind me of the symbols from that cult I almost joined while I was hitchhiking across the country. And I've never seen someone light literally dozens of candles for a bath. All of these clues make me think she's not a normal girl. Figuring out who she is is my new project.

I'm going to take a break from my blog for a while. I need some time to collect my thoughts on my own. No offense, I love you guys but I just need some "Kendra time".

So for now: "The end."

Free e-book: Read The Cornfield Creeps to find out how Kendra was exiled from her hometown!

"I never thought telling a scary story could get me in so much trouble.

I was just trying to be a good writing teacher and keep the children in my class awake—by scaring the crap out of them. What do you expect? I'm a horror writer, after all.

But then things got weird, real weird. Don't they always with me?"

Plus more short stories by Eve! Click the link below to get your copy FREE!

http://eveharms.com/cornfield-creeps-hell.html

About the Author

Eve Harms is a writer of freaky fun dark fiction and lover of esoteric knowledge. Her work has appeared in publications such as Vastarien Literary Journal, under Rayna Waxhead, and Creepy Catalog, under Kendra Temples. She currently resides in Los Angeles with her children's book illustrator spouse and two cats. You can connect with her on twitter and instagram under the handle @eveharmswrites and eveharms.com

Dear Reader, Please consider leaving a review

Thank you so much for reading HELLCRAFTER. If you enjoyed it, please leave a quick review on Amazon and/or Goodreads. Your review will help other readers like you find my work, and it would mean the world to me.

Yours,
Eve

Content Warnings

Hellcrafter includes graphic violence, themes of grief and trauma, loss of a loved one, body horror, insect horror, drug use, death of an animal, and sex.

Made in the USA
Middletown, DE
21 September 2023